E   Turner, Ann   c2
Tur   Warren.
          Dakota dugout

4650.   DATE DUE   PERMA-BOUND

Bust			
MAR 4 1991 C			
MAR. 18 1993			
T14			
OCT. 6 1994			

E   c2
Tur   Turner, Ann Warren

     Dakota dugout.

Ann Turner

DAKOTA DUGOUT

Illustrated by

Ronald Himler

discard

Aladdin Books

Macmillan Publishing Company · New York

Aladdin Books
Macmillan Publishing Company
866 Third Avenue, New York, NY 10022
Collier Macmillan Canada, Inc.
First Aladdin Books edition 1989
Printed in the United States of America
A hardcover edition of *Dakota Dugout* is available from
Macmillan Publishing Company.

10   9   8   7   6   5   4   3   2   1

Library of Congress Cataloging in Publication Data
Turner, Ann Warren.
Dakota dugout.
Summary: A woman describes her experiences living
with her husband in a sod house on the Dakota prairie.
1. Children's stories, American. [1. Frontier and
pioneer life—Fiction. 2. Great Plains—Fiction]
I. Himler, Ronald, ill. II. Title.
PZ7.T8535Dak   1989   [E]   85-3084
ISBN 0-689-71296-0 (pbk.)

For Rick, with love

*T*ell you about the prairie years?
I'll tell you, child, how it was.

When Matt wrote, "Come!"
I packed all I had,
cups and pots and dresses and rope,
even Grandma's silver boot hook,

and rode the clickety train
to a cave in the earth,
Matt's cave.

Built from sod, you know,
with a special iron plow
that sliced the long earth strips.

Matt cut them into bricks,
laid them up, dug into a hill
that was our first home.

I cried when I saw it.

No sky came in that room,
only a paper window
that made the sun look greasy.

Dirt fell on our bed,
snakes sometimes, too,
and the buffalo hide door
could not keep out the wind
or the empty cries in the long grass.

The birds visited me,
there was no one else,
with Matt all day in the fields.
A hawk came, snake in its claws,

a heron flapped by with wings like sails,
and a sparrow jabbered the day long
on a gray fence post.
I jabbered back.

Winter came sudden.
Slam-bang! the ground was iron,
cattle breath turned to ice,
froze their noses to the ground.

We lost twelve in a storm
and the wind scoured the dugout,
whish-hush, *whish*-hush.

Spring, child, was teasing slow
then quick,
water booming in the lake,
geese like yarn in the sky,

green spreading faster than fire,
and the wind blowing
shoosh-hush, *shoosh*-hush.

First summer we watched the corn grow,
strode around the field clapping hands.
We saw dresses, buggies, gold in that grain

until one day a hot wind baked it dry
as an oven, *ssst-ssst, ssst-ssst*.

Matt sat and looked two whole days,
silent and long.

Come fall we snugged like beavers
in our burrow, new grass on the floor,
willows our roof under the earth.

I pasted newspaper on the walls,
set bread to bake on the coals,
and the wind was quiet.

Corn grew finally,
we got our dresses, buggies, some gold,

built a clapboard house
with windows like suns,
floors I slipped on,
and the empty sound of too many rooms.

Didn't think I'd miss
the taste of earth in the air.
Now the broom went *whisp*-hush,
and the clock tocked like a busy heart.

Talking brings it near again,
the sweet taste of new bread
in a Dakota dugout,

how the grass whispered like an old friend,
how the earth kept us warm.

Sometimes the things we start with
are best.